Wondrously Made

By
Jessica Jones and Susan Samuels

Quiddity Press & Productions
Abbotsford, BC

Wondrously Made

By Jessica Jones and Susan Samuels

Published by
>Quiddity Press & Productions
>P.O. Box 1654, Sumas, WA 98295 U.S.A.

Any resemblance of names or places to actual events or locales, any persons, living or dead, is entirely coincidental.

First Printing 2009.
Printed in the United States of America

Quiddity Press & Productions
P.O. Box 1654
Sumas, WA 98295 U.S.A.

Publisher's Cataloging-In-Publication
(Provided by Quiddity Press & Publications)

Jones, Jessica; Samuels, Susan. – 1st ed.

LCCN:
ISBN-13: 978-0-9814548-0-1
ISBN-10: 0-9814548-0-1

INDEX

"And they shall rebuild the old ruins, they shall raise up the former desolations, and they shall repair the ruined cities, the desolations of many generations."—Isaiah 61:4

FORWARD

My life has been plagued by medical interventions and physical onslaughts from birth. My mother's doctor miscalculated the time of gestation and, to suit his schedule, I was prematurely "delivered" via C-section. From there, my health went downhill with diabetes, pneumonia, bronchitis, hypoglycemia, rheumatoid arthritis, simple arthritis, osteoarthritis, tinnitus, cancer (skin and cervical), and the list goes on. A book could be filled with the symptoms of the various ailments and pain that has plagued my body. And more recently added to the list was fibromyalgia and irritable bowel syndrome.

My youth was overwhelmed with sickness and pain, which got mildly more tolerable with age.

At last count, and there will be no more, I have undergone 35 surgeries in total including bilateral patellectomies, bilateral Carpal Tunnel, hysterectomy, fundoplication, etc.

Physically, my life has been a mess. However, a lifetime of poor health and torturous existence was not God's plan for me. He is a God of good gifts (James 1:17) and eternal life (Romans 6:23), neither of which I was enjoying. It was hard to rationalize my situation in light of these scriptures.

I once belonged to the school of thought that God would heal me of my sufferings in His time, when He got around to it, or when He finished teaching me what I needed to learn through these illnesses, but I could not find this sentiment in the scriptures.

These wrong teachings came straight from the pulpit. However, I soon realized that it is our responsibility to search out the answers for ourselves in God's own word, the Bible.

He has provided all we need for complete health and healing. He has provided us with nourishing food, life-giving water and everything we need to heal ourselves. This includes a miraculous body equipped with the amazing ability to heal itself. He has given us all we need. "By His stripes we are healed...." (Isaiah 53:5)

I needed to find the meaning of those words. I needed to find the way to His better plan. My search began to determine what was of God and what was not, what was true and was not.

I looked into the various methods available to regain health.

I needed to find what would restore me to health without raping my wallet or the land. It also had to be uncomplicated. I'm just not interested in methods that require huge chunks of my day just to implement the plan. That cannot be right.

There is something inherently wrong with the concept of using large amounts of plant, animal or sea creatures to make concentrated juices, capsules or pills. And I didn't want to have to spend money indefinitely on pills, potions or treatments that simply didn't last.

I have tried so many things in my life. Homeopathy held little success for me. Naturopathic doctors fed me uncountable bottles of a dark brown liquid which tasted horridly bitter and didn't fix the current problems. The treatment lasted for years with no end in sight. I have tried acupuncturists in both North America and China with little relief or change to my health.

I have tried countless potions from Chinese herbalists, resulting in yet another hospital visit with irritated stomach problems. Prescribed medicines simply kept the symptoms at bay for awhile; but they usually came back with a vengeance... plus some side effects. In my desperate attempts to gain relief, I had 35 surgeries which only aggravated the problems. They simply removed one problem while creating new ones.

I have gone to chiropractors for over forty years. Again, it is never over - you have to return every week or month to repeatedly adjust your back or relocate your jaw from chronic TMJ. It was a miserable existence that made me feel years older than my true age.

Everything increased the problems, making me sicker or more crippled. I needed a change. I was ready to look into areas not previously considered.

My search took me not only to the available medical options but also included biblical research. This book is the result of that search. I believe it is the end of 56 years of searching for the truth. There was finally a light at the end of a very long and dark tunnel.

We are indeed wondrously made.

I have heard this and now am beginning to believe it. It was very hard to verify by the way I felt. There was a big discrepancy between the way we are supposed to be and the way I was. I needed a major attitude correction to realize the truth. He created me to be pain free, disease free and full of health. But my reality was far from this truth. Before I could even enter into that arena, I needed a change in my thinking. So began my search.

We are made in the image of God and He has written His glory all over our being. But what does that mean?

God speaks volumes to us throughout the Bible by using names and numbers and it is our honor to search out the deep meanings and how they apply.

Our body design displays the love of God through the numbers written into our very code. God is very mathematical and everything in the universe portrays His glory through the meaning of these numbers.

We were not created to suffer, to be riddled with disease, or tormented by looming death sentences. I received my two-year death sentence one year ago. Little attention was paid to it until recently when it dawned on me that one of those two years had already passed. Now, with one year left, I am not only attentive but am determined to make long overdue radical changes.

This search has included every aspect of healthy living, but from God's perspective, not man's agenda. I want to show you how the design and function of our body (the city of God), lines up with the design and function of His city of Jerusalem, as well as the tribes of Israel. I hope you enjoy the revelation of my search and let it speak to you, so you too can find your way back to the health the Creator desires for you.

CHAPTER 1: THE CITY OF GOD

The first city of God was technically the encampment in the wilderness when the Israelites set their tents around the tabernacle of God. The tabernacle was the temple in the wilderness.

Jerusalem became the city of God after the Ark of the Covenant was installed into the tabernacle during the reign of King David. This may seem like another Bible story, but it is pertinent to understanding just who we are, what God desires for us and what He created us to be. It is exciting to bear the honor God has built into our bodies.

The tabernacle in the wilderness had no gates. It was not until Israel conquered Canaan and took Jerusalem that the city of God was built, complete with gates. It was a jewel in the desert and lay at the heart of every Israelite's affections. Songs were sung about it. And each year every male Israelite was instructed to visit Jerusalem.

And within the gates, within the tabernacle, the Lord of Hosts sat upon the Mercy Seat in the Holy of Holies.

Before it became the jewel of the Israelites, Jerusalem was called Salem, a city ruled by King Melchizedek during the time of Abraham. Melchizedek was the priest of the Most High who brought communion, bread and wine, to Abraham on his return from war in which Abraham saved the kings of the plain and rescued his nephew, Lot.

During the reign of the Israelites, Jerusalem had eleven gates. Ten gates are found in Nehemiah 3:3-31 during the rebuilding of the city after the Israelites return from Babylonian captivity, and the eleventh is found in Jeremiah 37:13.

The gates were listed counter-clockwise. They were the Sheep, Fish, Old, Valley, Dung, Fountain, Water, Horse, East, Inspection and Benjamin. This is the same counter-clockwise order that becomes apparent in the steps of our Christian walk as we grow and mature in all the ways of the Lord.

We will look at the meanings of the names of those who repaired the gates. If there are numbers of import, they also will be included in this brief examination with the meanings in parenthesis directly behind the number.

As an example, I have had 35 (*hope*) operations and I am 56 years old (56 = 50 (*freedom, jubilee*) + 6 (*number of man, weakness of man, inventions of man*)). Broken down, this means there is finally <u>hope</u> for the <u>freedom</u> from the <u>inventions and weakness of man</u>. I am finally on the road of hope, not despair.

Let's look at the gates of Jerusalem.

The Sheep Gate was repaired by Eliashib (*the God of Conversion*), the high priest, along with his fellow priests. This was the gate through which the sheep and goats were brought into the city to be sacrificed. It was the only gate of the eleven that was sanctified. It is at this gate that you will find the Pool of Bethesda (House of Mercy; flowing water) of John 5 where Jesus healed an infirm man. It was this pool that was stirred by the finger of an angel.

There, a man suffering an infirmity for 38 (*slavery*) years could never get into the pool quickly enough to be first and therefore the one to be healed. Jesus asked him, "Do you want to be well?" This man was a slave to infirmity, a cruel and unceasing taskmaster. It was at the House of Mercy that this man received his release from slavery.

We become so accustomed to a life of infirmity until we hear the voice of the One who loves us and desires to release us from our slavery. He does not hesitate to say "Pick up your mat and walk into the temple and enjoy the Sabbath, the rest of the Lord." The House of Mercy is for both the new and the old *sheep* of the Lord. Whether we are new Christians or have been Christians most of our lives, we can still answer the call and enter into the Sheep Gate to receive our healing at the pool of Bethesda.

The Fish Gate was repaired by the brothers of Hassenaah (*Hated One*). It was the place of commerce where the fishermen brought their catch to sell. The Fish Gate was known for its corruption and Zephaniah gave a prophetic warning to the people because of their sin there. But Jesus said He would make His people fishers of men. Corruption would end and His sheep would no longer serve Mammon, or corrupt commerce. They would serve the living God in freedom, health and liberty, giving away that same freedom, health and liberty to others.

The Old Gate was built by two friends, Joida (w*hom God favors)*, son of Paseah (*son of the Passover)*, and Meshullam (*peace*), son of Besodiah (*the secret of the Lord*). It is the Old Gate that represents the foundations of our faith, the wisdom and understanding upon which our faith is built. Here is where we find the favor of the Lord that causes the Angel of Death to pass over us. It is at the Old Gate where we find the peace that surpasses all understanding in the secrets of the Lord. It is at the Old Gate where we find the foundations of our faith in the Godhead and Their unfathomable love for us. It is at the Old Gate where we find the truths of the Bible as revealed to us by the Lord. Ask and it shall be given to you; seek and you shall find; knock and it shall be opened unto you. (Luke 11:9 NKJV)

The next gate to be repaired was the Valley Gate, also repaired by friends. It was built by Hanun (*gracious, merciful*), and the residents of Zanoah (*cast off*). The valley in scripture is often associated with the place of trials, tribulations and sorrow. After running on the highs of the mountaintop experiences, we all enter the valley experience when we feel abandoned in our hardships. But the valley is the place where vegetation grows which represents the place where our faith grows and our walk becomes more surefooted. It is where we learn to hold onto the Lord, believing that He cares enough to see us through. It is the place where He is gracious and merciful even though we feel thrown aside and outcast. It is in the valleys that we strengthen our character and learn He is worthy of our trust. It is in the valley where we find out just how much He does love and care for us.

The Dung Gate is the place where we remove the garbage and refuse from the city into the pit outside. It was repaired by one man, Malchiah (*my king is Yahweh*), son of Rechab (*rider*), ruler of Bethhaccerem (*house of the vineyard*). How could a man with such a name and lineage be the repairer of the Dung Gate? It is perhaps the most important gate of the city. Without this gate, the city would have quickly become a cesspool of refuse and contamination. The Dung Gate represents deliverance in our lives where we can take the garbage out and be clean. It is the job of the Holy Spirit to spotlight the garbage in our lives which needs to be removed. Malchiah was a man delivered from the garbage and baggage of his ancestral line so that his king truly was Yahweh, the mighty rider from the house of the vineyard! He did not look at the garbage; he looked at the greatness of his God. Deliverance keeps our city clean. The Dung Gate is the symbol of the Holy Spirit in our lives and of His work as promised in Exodus 23:28. He will chase out our enemies from the bushes for us so we can get rid of them, carting the garbage outside the city walls and dropping them into the pit.

The Fountain Gate was repaired by Shallun (*retribution*), son of Colhozeh (*all-seeing*), ruler of Mizpah (*watchtower*). Here he rebuilt the pool of Shiloah (*sent*) by the king's garden. The Pool of Shiloah brought water under the city from the river of Siloam. This water supply saved the city against many enemy sieges. In a time of retribution from enemies, the all-seeing God stands as a watchtower over His people bringing them life-giving, healing waters. After our deliverance, we need to stand in the everlasting healing waters of Jesus to wash away that which was just cleaned out at the Dung Gate. Here we find the Fountain of Life (Psalm 36:9), the Fountain of Gardens (Song of Solomon 4:15) and the Fountain of Living Waters (Jeremiah 2:13). But it is also the Fountain of Tears (Jeremiah 9:1) where we weep for the slain of God's people, the ones who do not know the way to freedom but stay bound to the yoke of slavery.

The Water Gate was repaired by the temple slaves. These slaves were Gibeonites assigned to the Levites in perpetuity to be water bearers by Joshua in payment for their deception. The Gibeonites were Amorites, enemies of Israel. The city of Gibeon, where the sun stood still in Israel's war against the Amorites and where David conquered the Philistines, was given to the Levites. The Water Gate is the sign of forgiveness and repentance. The Water Gate was the ritual bath used once a year by the High Priest where he cleansed himself for the Day of Atonement. On the other side of the gate was the Lishkat Antinus, the room where the incense offered on the

Golden Alter was mixed. This is the gate of forgiveness, repentance and prayer as the Holy Spirit washes us clean with the living water, the Word, and the Father smells the sweet fragrance of our prayers. He forgives us of our transgressions, our deceptions, and, instead of defeating us, He pardons us and hears our prayers.

The next gate, the Horse Gate, was repaired by the priests who lived around the gate. Horses represent discipline, strength, endurance and speed. It speaks of service. A horse that is broken and disciplined is a horse that can be used to pull a cart, carry a messenger or be ridden to war. The horse knows his master intimately and responds to the slightest nuance of movement by hand, knee or foot. The horse is also the sign of judgment as seen in Revelation 19:11. This is the time when we judge ourselves lest we be judged; we can return to the Water Gate in repentance and prayer to be forgiven, cleansed and watered.

Next is the East Gate built by the guards Zadok (righteous), son of Immer (he hath said), and Shemaiah (heard by Yahweh), keeper of the East Gate. As the Lord has spoken, this gate was built in righteousness for the return of the King. The Lord has heard the decree and ordered this gate to be repaired while shut. Ezekiel 44:1-3 tells us that it is the gate used by the Lord and no one else. This gate represents the coming of the Lord. In John 20:26 the verse suggests that Jesus walked through the closed doors to stand in the midst of the disciples just as He will return through the closed gate. It represents the coming

Messiah who will return, riding down from heaven, commander of the heavenly armies through the gate of the dimensions, from the heavenly realm to the natural realm. It is the promise and declaration that Jesus, our King will return as Lord of lords.

The second to last gate is the Inspection Gate. It is here, at this gate, that the sheep are separated from the goats. It is the gate of Judgment and division where one is either judged worthy to be a sheep, and passes onto the final gate, or is judged as a goat and sent to prison or hell. It was repaired by the goldsmith's son, Malchiah (my king is Yahweh). Gold is the symbol of the nature of the Father. The fact that this gate was repaired by the goldsmith's son speaks to us of the Father's Son who is to be our judge. Jesus is God and there is no other like Him. He alone is judge, not you or I. The final decision is His. Only one man repaired the Inspection Gate as only one God will be judge. Matthew 25:34-35, 41-42 tells of those accepted to be blessed and those who were commanded to depart. It is the gate of division, everyone in the city was separated into two camps: saved or lost, free or condemned.

The final gate is not found in Nehemiah and was not actually repaired by the people. It is only found in Jeremiah 37:13 and the actual location or information of this gate is somewhat forgotten and vague. However, Jeremiah tells us that it is the Gate of Benjamin. This gate was so called, because it faces the tribe of Benjamin, famed for causing a civil war within the tribes of Israel and becoming almost extinct as a result. This is the gate that stands as a reminder of the civil war between the children of God and it bears a warning. Woe to them who cause division in the camp of God, for they too will be cut off. We are all the children of God, created with an inheritance and a purpose to be a child of God, the son of God, the Bride of Christ. But look around. We are in a civil war with our brothers. We are not the unified people who are known for their love, unfortunately. We are all children of Adam and Eve, and yet, even though every person on earth is related, we are in a civil war with our brothers. Zechariah 14:8-11; Job 19:25-26; Psalm 68:29; Isaiah 18:7, 24:23; Daniel 7:27; Joel 3:16-21; 2 Timothy 2:12 and; Revelation 5:10, 12:5, 19:15 and 20:4-6 tell us that this gate is New Jerusalem...a new heaven and a new earth created for the people of God. Like New Jerusalem, it is not a city or gate repaired by man but by God alone.

In summary the gates represent:
1. SHEEP—healing/salvation
2. FISH—release from corruption and serving Mammon
3. OLD—a firm foundation to build a new life
4. VALLEY—trials to stretch and grow in faith and hope
5. DUNG—deliverance of the garbage (sin/demonic spirits) in our lives
6. FOUNTAIN—cleansing and filling after being delivered
7. WATER—forgiveness after the Lord has heard our prayers of repentance

8. HORSE—discipline and training for Kingdom life
9. EAST—the hope and promise that Christ will return
10. INSPECTION—inspected and found worthy as sheep and not a goat
11. BENJAMIN—the hope and promise of New Jerusalem and eternity

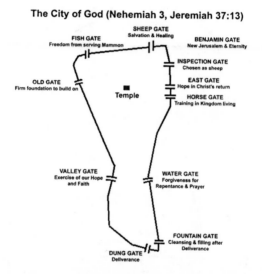

The City of God (Nehemiah 3, Jeremiah 37:13)

We are created in the form of this city. We are the city of God. I am not just taking a blind leap here, using symbolism to make a point. The Bible calls us the temple of God and the Holy Spirit dwells within us. That is, if we are Christians, having accepted Jesus' sacrifice, the price of our sins is paid. But even more dramatic, and exciting, I will show you how we are the city of God and a reflection of Jerusalem.

The City of God (Nehemiah 3, Jeremiah 37:13)

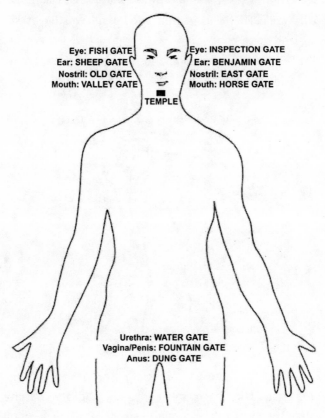

Jerusalem, the City of God has eleven gates. Our bodies have 11 gates.

We have two ears, two eyes and two nostrils. The mouth contains two channels (one to stomach and one to lungs). We have one urethra, vagina (female)/penis (male) and anus. All our gates total 11.

These 11 gates of our bodies line up with the gates of Jerusalem. Going counter-clockwise as did Nehemiah, our 11 gates are: ear, eye, nostril, mouth (to stomach), anus, vagina/penis, urethra, mouth (to lungs), nostril, eye, and ear. Why did Nehemiah go counter-clockwise? We were created to be eternal.

1. We hear the Master's voice to enter the SHEEP Gate—the ear gate.
2. We see the truth and become FISHers of men—the eye gate.
3. We breathe deeply of the OLD Foundations to build our faith—the nostril.
4. We cry in the VALLEY of sorrows and call out to God to help us and teach us the lessons we must learn—the mouth to stomach gate.
5. We carry the DUNG/garbage/ baggage out of our lives through deliverance—the anus gate.
6. We bring forth life from the FOUNTAIN of life as did Mary who birthed the Son through the grace of the Holy Spirit—the vagina/penis gate.
7. The urethra is our WATER Gate that filters out the fluids in our bodies and cleanses us continually.
8. The mouth channel that goes to our lungs holds the bit of discipline and training that the HORSE wears as it is being broken for service.

9. There is a fresh wind coming from the EAST Gate as we breath in deeply of the hope and anticipation of the sweet savor of our coming Lord and Savior—the 2nd nostril gate.

10. We must view ourselves with an honest eye in all truth so that we judge ourselves lest we be judged so that everything is placed under the feet of Jesus and covered by the blood of Christ—the INSPECTION gate.

11. We must hear the voice of our Lord and Savior with our ear instead of the tumult of civil war behind us so that we can enter into New Jerusalem with love and unity as a new heaven and earth are created—the BENJAMIN gate.

❧ ❧

ELEVEN TRIBES are also represented around the tabernacle in the wilderness in the Pentateuch. Manasseh and Ephraim represent Joseph and, for this purpose, are considered one: Joseph. But they represent two generations in our lives as Joseph's sons.

1. Naphtali (*wrestling*) is the first tribe listed. He represents the Sheep Gate where we enter into the safety of salvation from a life of wrestling with ourselves and against God. It represents the ceaseless struggle to make life better on our own terms. And it

reminds us that our way simply does not work but leaves an emptiness deep within our spirit regardless what degree of "success" we may achieve in the natural world.

2. Reuben (*behold a son*) is the second tribe. It represents a new God to follow, not the miserable taskmaster of Mammon. It is the Fish Gate where we hear and see the Lord and He tells us to leave our trade of fish mongering and follow Him to become fishers of men.

3. Gad (*Good Fortune*) is the third tribe mentioned. There is good fortune to be found in the Old Gate, for it is the Old Ways that are the foundation of our salvation, the foundation for abundant life. It is the return to the Old Ways that will help us stand firm and strong in our faith. It is the return to the Old Ways that will make us rich, not the pursuit of money.

4. Benjamin (*son of my right hand*) is next and represents the Valley Gate. Regardless of the trials, sorrows and tribulations set before us, we must remember that Jesus is Lord and that we are the son of His right hand. We must remember who we are in Christ, the Son of God. We must not forget who we are and who our Father is, lest we enter into division and civil war.

5. Joseph (one who gathers; Y*ahweh has added*) envelopes two roles through his sons, both Manasseh (*causing to forget*) and Ephraim (*double ash-heap, I*

shall be doubly fruitful) as representatives of the Dung Gate. Joseph stands for *one who gathers or one who increases*. How better can one describe deliverance but one who gathers the garbage and takes it outside the camp to the pit, thereby increasing his space and dwelling area. And as Manasseh we deliver our city of the ancient ancestral spirits from our lives, plus, represented by the younger son, the spirits we personally allowed to affect our lives in this generation. The tribe of Joseph through his two sons embraces the entire scope of deliverance.

6. Zebulun (*exalted*) represents the Fountain Gate, our dwelling place. For this is the gate that represents the Baptism of the Holy Spirit who causes us to be exalted as His dwelling place, hence we become the temple of the Lord, filling the places vacated by the spirits that had taken over our lives, but are now delivered to the pit.

7. Judah (*praised*) represents the Water Gate, a place of forgiveness, repentance, prayer and praise for our deliverance, where we wash in the word of God, continually cleansing ourselves.

8. Issachar (*there is recompense*) represents the Horse Gate, the animal of servitude to our Master with the promise of recompense for our servitude. What is our recompense? The promise of a returning King who will judge us and find us worthy to go into New

Jerusalem. He represents the discipline and training in our lives so that we can honestly, with respect and love, enter into a life of servitude to the Master of our lives who holds the bit in our mouths in His hand.

9. Asher (*happy*) represents the praise and anticipation of the East Gate as we await the coming of the Lord once again.

10. Dan (*a judge*) represents the Inspection Gate where the goats and the sheep are separated for their individual judgments. The goats are sent to the Lake of Fire while the sheep are reserved for New Jerusalem.

11. Simeon (heard) represents the hearing children in the final civil war of Armageddon who hear and follow the voice of the Lamb through the gate of Benjamin into the city of New Jerusalem for eternity as it was shown to John in the book of Revelation.

The gates represent the path of the Christian life, both physically and spiritually. We are the city of God with eleven gates. We were created to be the gleaming gem in this desert of lies and hopelessness, this earthly desert of despair in which we live. And just as in the city eleven things happened at the gates, we are to abound in the things of God, being the very gates that allow or refuse entry:

1. Wisdom utters her voice at the gates (Proverbs 24:7). We are to be vessels of wisdom.

2. Courts of justice were held (Deuteronomy 16:18). We

are to be vessels of justice and mercy.

3. Land was redeemed. Our land is to be redeemed and we are to help redeem the land of others.

4. Proclamations and declarations were made (Jeremiah 17:19-20). We are to walk in the authority of who we are in Christ.

5. Councils of state were held (2 Chronicles 18:9). We are to walk in kingdom life of ruling and reigning.

6. Public commendations were made (Proverbs 31:23). We are not to tear others down but to build them up, restoring them unto the Lord.

7. Gates were shut at night. We are to rest in the Lord and His safety and take time to heal.

8. Gates were a primary target during war (Ezekiel 21:22). Our gates need to be guarded at all times. We are not to be unwary of the attacks against us from without or within, but stand firm, fighting not against flesh and blood, but against principalities, powers, rulers of darkness of this age, and spiritual hosts in heavenly places. (Ezekiel 6:12)

9. Gates were razed or burned to gain entry (Zechariah 2:5). We are not to be unwary of the enemy's devices and plans but to stand strong against every attack so we will overcome and stand.

10. Acts of idolatry happened (Acts 14:13). We are not to allow idolatry to enter through our gates, but like Israel declare, "The Lord my God is one!"

11. Experienced officers were placed over gates. We

must be under authority to be in authority.

But there is more. We not only have eleven gates, we have eleven bodily systems reinforcing how we are made in the likeness of the City of God, proving that we are the City of God.

1. The Muscular system consists of 3 subsystems:
   a. muscles
   b. tendons
   c. ligaments
2. The Skeletal system consists of 3 subsystems:
   a. bone
   b. cartilage
   c. joints
3. The Cardiovascular system consists of 3 subsystems:
   a. heart
   b. blood
   c. vessels
4. The Digestive system consists of 14 subsystems: (2 x 7... witness perfection)
   a. mouth
   b. pharynx
   c. esophagus
   d. stomach
   e. intestines
   f. rectum
   g. anal canal
   h. teeth
   i. salivary glands
   j. tongue
   k. liver

     l. gallbladder
     m. pancreas
     n. appendix
5. The Endocrine system consists of 10 subsystems (2 x 5... witness grace)
     a. pituitary gland
     b. pineal body
     c. hypothalamus
     d. thyroid gland
     e. parathyroid gland
     f. thymus gland
     g. adrenal glands
     h. pancreas
     i. ovaries
     j. testes
6. The Integumentary system consists of 6 subsystems: (3 x 2...witness completion)
     a. skin
     b. hair
     c. nails
     d. sense receptors
     e. sweat glands
     f. oil glands
7. The Urinary system consists of 4 subsystems:
     a. kidneys
     b. ureters
     c. bladder
     d. urethra
8. The Lymphatic system consists of 4 subsystems:
     a. lymph nodes
     b. lymphatic vessels
     c. thymus gland

    d. spleen

9. The Respiratory system consists of 6 subsystems:
   a. nose
   b. pharynx
   c. larynx
   d. trachea
   e. bronchi
   f. lungs

10. The Nervous system consists of 3 subsystems:
   a. brain
   b. spinal cord
   c. nerves

11. The Reproductive system consists of 6 male subsystems and 7 Female subsystems:

a.	testes	(M)
b.	vas deferens	(M)
c.	urethra	(M) (F)
d.	prostate gland	(M)
e.	penis	(M)
f.	scrotum	(M)
g.	ovaries	(F)
h.	uterus	(F)
i.	uterine tubes	(F)
j.	vagina	(F)
k.	external genital organs	(F)
l.	mammary glands	(F)

❧ ☙

The positive meaning of the number eleven stands for 1 + 1, or 2, which represents double witness, the keepers of *something* (the woman, the temple, and the elect). And as the woman, the Bride of Christ, the human body (both male and female) has eleven gates (orifices) that leave and enter our bodies.

We are the keepers of the Holy Spirit who dwells within us. If we do not have the Holy Spirit through the salvation of Jesus Christ, we move in the negative meaning of the number 11 (disorder), because we are not keepers of something. We are in essence, empty.

We would be, in effect, Jezebel, the woman who would be queen without the power of God. She wanted the position on her own terms and with her own gods. But it does not work that way.

The city of God was complete, as we are complete, only with the temple of God within it/us. Levi, the priests of God, maintains the temple of God. We will go more into that in a later chapter.

We were created to be a gleaming bright city, a shining example of God in the natural dimension. We were created without spot or wrinkle, but our forefathers fell into sin in the Garden of Eden. So, instead of that gleaming city that is to be a light unto the world, we are more like the city of God after it had been decimated by Nebuchadnezzar and destroyed. So many of us cannot walk, are riddled with disease, aches and pains, and life is a miserable existence at best aided by the thin veneer of band-aids; surgery, drugs and various "alternate" methods to mask symptoms instead of healing the problem.

But to use the city of God, Jerusalem, as our example, you will notice that the repairs came from inside the city. There was no raping the land. No one dug into their pockets, scrambling to heal and repair of the city. They used what was available repairing the city to the former gleaming emblem of the Lord in the desert of despair. They fought the rebukes and ridicule of those around them, remaining true to their convictions and raised the city up from within. The people who repaired the city from within were allowed to return home from exile.

We have exiled our repairers by turning to drugs, abuses, excesses, addictions, and alternate forms of medicine. Our first response is to scramble to anything else, instead of letting God be God and our bodies be the cities they were designed to be. Let us look into who the repairers are and how we can bring them back from exile.

God has stamped His life upon us and shown His great love for us in every part of our makeup...His creation.

This is such an important message that it bears repeating. The body was designed to heal itself...if we allow those responsible for the repairs to return to their work.

CHAPTER 2: THE INNER WORKINGS

As said above, the numbers of God are stamped all over our body. We have 11 gates and 11 systems. Those 11 systems are divided into 5 groups.

1. The Muscular, Skeletal, Cardiovascular and Nervous systems each consist of 3 parts, as listed in the previous chapter.
2. The Digestive system consists of 14 parts, listed in the previous chapter.
3. The Endocrine system consists of 9 parts, as listed in the previous chapter.
4. The Integumentary, Respiratory and Reproductive systems each consist of 6 parts, as listed in the previous chapter.
5. The Urinary and Lymphatic systems each consist of 4 parts, as listed in the previous chapter.

As we have seen, the 11 (*keepers of something*) systems are divided into 5 (*grace, protection, peace*) different sections, just like the spine is divided into 5 different sections.

If you take the sum of all the parts of the 11 systems, you come up to a total of 53 parts in the 11 (*keepers of something*) systems.

Take away the number of the 33 (*promise*) vertebrae from

the total number of 53 parts in the 11 systems and you are left with the 28 (*eternal life*) parts. 33 stands for *promise*, 28 stands for *eternal life* and 5 stands for God's grace, peace and protection.

In other words, we have, through God's grace, peace and protection the double promise of eternal life. As we saw in the previous chapter, the human body, like the city of Jerusalem, is designed to heal itself indefinitely.

But let's look at the different sections and see what we find.

The first section is 4 (*creation*) systems of 3 (*perfection*) parts: Muscular, Skeletal, Cardiovascular and Nervous. God is telling us that we are perfect in our creation.

The Digestive system consists of 14 (*deliverance, salvation*) parts. There is only 1 deliverance and salvation for mankind —not many ways as has been suggested.

The Endocrine system consists of 9 parts (*judgment, the physical manifestation of the fruit of understanding*). The Endocrine system actually communicates with and controls all the mechanisms of the body. This tells us that if we willingly step under judgment we shall have the fruit of the understanding poured out onto us. Instead of fearing conviction, we should embrace it because along with repentance comes the gift of forgiveness, the under-standing of our sin and a change of heart.

There are 3 (*perfection*) systems with 6 (*number of man*) parts. Man was created perfect in his being.

And finally, there are 2 (*witness*) systems with 4 (*creation*) parts. Our creation is a witness to the goodness of God.

God has stamped His glory all over our creation. Let's put it all together. We have, through God's grace, peace and protection the double promise of eternal life. This is manifested both spiritually through the gift of life through the cross, and physically because the human body is designed to heal itself indefinitely. We are perfect in our creation. There is only one way to deliverance and salvation for mankind. If we willingly step under judgment we shall have the fruit of the understanding poured out onto us. Man was created perfect in his being and our creation is a witness to the goodness of God.

We were created in the image of God.

Forget the doom and gloom religious spirits that say we have to be forced into a Christian walk of pain and sickness to identify with Christ. It is done! Let's rejoice in the freedom and liberty the Lord has provided for us. Life is to be a celebration of joy to the Lord, not drudgery and misery.

The freedom He died to restore to us is there for the taking. It is a walk into liberty, a freedom from sorrow, illness, disease, hardship and slavery. We are perfect in our creation as a witness to the goodness of God... not a cruel or ill-tempered

God, but a good God. Nothing about our creation suggests a God that doesn't want the complete best for us.

In fact, Song of Solomon 7:10 tells us in joyful excitement and with shouting, "I am my Beloved's and His desire is towards me!"

I am His! I belong to Him! He is the Creator of all life and I belong to Him! And He desires me all the time. He wants me. He longs to be with me. He loves me. He has chosen me to be His!

If His desire is towards me 24/7, His desire is not that I be broken, sick and subjected to 35 (*hope*) surgeries resulting in missing parts. His desire is not for me to be crippled, in agonizing pain, ill health and miserable. His desire is that I be full of health and full enjoyment of life—the life He died to give me.

Our calling is to be the Bride of Christ. What husband wants a broken, crippled, sack of misery as His bride? I haven't met any. That is why He died to give us health, joy and peace. That is why He sacrificed His life so we could have one. Not a life of drudgery and agony, but joy, liberty and peace.

Which life do you have? I know which life I had. And I knew it was time for an upgrade. It was time to accept all of Jesus' sacrifice, and not leave Him hanging on the cross because I only wanted part of what he was offering. It was time to apply it to my life personally. It was time to start living a victorious life instead of one filled with defeat.

Finally, I can say, after 35 unhelpful and even harmful surgeries, I now have the hope for a new way, God's way, out of ill-health, into renewed health and restoration.

However, there is still something wrong with this picture. I am not who He created me to be. Far from the perfect city of God, I am that city after the destruction by the Babylonians. I am broken down and in ill repair before the Israelites returned from exile to rebuild the city. My team needs to be called back from their captivity in a strange land so they can be allowed to repair my city from within.

Who can repair my city? Who can make me strong and whole again, able to withstand any attacks from my enemies? Where do I find the workers?

How did I get to be broken? How do any of us get to be so broken? I think we need to look at the story of the Babylonians and Israel. We find the story in 2 Chronicles 31 and 2 Kings 20:12-21.

Hezekiah, King of Judah, had a problem with pride. The Lord saved him from the Babylonian enemies threatening to destroy Judah, but Hezekiah wanted the glory, the credit, for himself. Hezekiah repented for his pride and the punishment was overturned. Instead, the Lord blessed Hezekiah abundantly for his humbleness. Everything King Hezekiah did was blessed and he became a very wealthy king indeed.

However, Hezekiah's pride rose to the forefront once again.

During an illness, an ambassador from Babylon brought the ailing king a gift. In return, Hezekiah showed the ambassador all the treasures of his kingdom, suggesting the increase was by his own hands. He showed this ambassador all the secret treasures of the temple including the spice and the ointment that was reserved for the kings and priests of the Most High God. He showed the ambassador all his weapons and military strength.

Hezekiah, pridefully bragging, displayed to the enemy the things that should have been kept secret.

Then, when confronted with his pride and the consequence of his sin, Hezekiah did not repent, but instead accepted the fate for his sons, provided his own life could be lived out in peace.

The destruction of Jerusalem and the rape of its temple and people was an inherited consequence because of the sin of pride in the king of Judah.

This leads me to look at my own illnesses. I was born with a very rare type of birthmark that will turn cancerous. It was a giant congenital melanocytic naevi. The spiritual root for cancer is long-term bitterness, hatred, anger, retaliation, helplessness, and broken relationship with God, others and self.

Could I have felt completely helpless as I was pulled from my mother 2 months prematurely. Could I have been bitter for the condition I soon found myself in—the blood transfusion, the isolated incubator? Could I have hated life so early and let bitterness in?

This disease was also inherited from my generations. I know this because it takes long-term bitterness to create cancer. And since no one else in my family had this disease in their bodies, it lies at the door of my parents.

Like King Mannaseh, who was hauled off to Babylon in bronze fetters and hooks in his nose, we shared the consequences of inherited sin. Both my father and mother had long-term bitterness. My father was sold into slavery to a farmer by his own mother when he was 9 (end of an age) years old. My grandfather was sold as an illegitimate newborn to a family emigrating from Ireland to Canada. Both shared long-term bitterness between them, and I inherited the consequences of their sin.

This is how the enemy entered my kingdom. And since it was the end of an age (meaning of the number 9) then I would find freedom and liberty in my life. I was designed to be born perfect and whole, but there was an enemy already in the kingdom. And according to the story of King Hezekiah, we can tell the nature of that enemy.

The enemies known as the Babylonians were God-mockers. They mocked the religious beliefs and practices of Israel. They spoke in the Israelites' own language to frighten them with feigned familiarity and the possibility of betrayal from within.

Our enemy is an enemy who mocks God and that means only one enemy—the fallen angels of heaven we now call spirits and demons.

Once these enemies gained entrance into the city, they stole every treasure, every weapon, every holy artifact and took captive every person. They destroyed the walls and gates, wreaking havoc on the city that was once the perfect city of God. They destroyed the temple of God leaving not one stone upon another.

This is the damage they have done to me. They have left me bereft of even my hope to see Jerusalem whole and beautiful again. They dragged me away to the land of disease and torment as a slave and a eunuch unable to bear children. But after 35 operations and 56 years, I now stood at the hope of my deliverance.

I looked at the lives of the Hebrews under the dominating rule of their Babylonian captors and came up with a eight-step plan that would rebuild my city. It was, in essence, how the Hebrews returned to their beloved Jerusalem and rebuilt it according to directions.

There are eight steps to total health, all of which encompass the pivotal center of life. We were created to be in relationship with the Father, Son and Holy Spirit, and outside that relationship we are not whole.

Second, a great deal of healing needs to be done because of the shame, oppression, traumas and lifestyle of being a prisoner in exile. Esther bathed for 6 months in a bath of myrrh which is an essential oil used for healing. She had to heal before she could even learn how to become queen.

Third, there must be deliverance from all the shackles, sin and unbelief that kept us in bondage. There must be a deliverance from all the things that would keep us connected to the enemy.

Pain resulting from the misalignment of the upper cervical vertebrae causes trauma which is one of the ways that provides an open door for demonic spirits to get a foothold in our life. Do not be deceived. Fears, stress, guilt, rejection and many, many more casually accepted reactions are all demonic spirits. "God did not give us a spirit of fear, but of power, love, and a sound mind..." (2 Timothy 1:7). And like the Dung Gate, God has made a way to clear this garbage out of our lives.

Upper cervical alignment ties into the fourth step. The temple of God must be restored so that we can once again hear the voice of God without disruption. If we are not hearing the word of God whisper to our inner being, perhaps the temple has not been restored.

We must get the pressure off the brain stem where it connects to the spinal cord. It is simple really, if your head is not on straight, or in alignment, then operating messages cannot flow freely throughout the rest of your body via the nerves because they are being pinched or compressed.

Fifth, we must make ourselves fit to once again live and work in the city. Exercise makes every cell in our bodies fit.

Regular exercise is essential in our 21st century lifestyle. It increases circulation and oxygen supply, loosens up joints, and relieves stress build up. There is no need to train for the Olympics or a triathlon, but a daily 30 minute brisk walk, or any program that you enjoy will achieve results.

Sixth, we need to provide our bodies with proper nutrition as a building block for replacing brokenness with whole and healthy bodies after a long exile in a foreign land of captors. This exchanges overindulgence and excessive abuse with the simple wisdom of nurturing our bodies God's way.

Seventh, we must be in community for no man is an island unto himself. We were created together, as family, as a body. We were created together to be the Bride of Christ. We were created to need each other, to help each other, the gifts being distributed amongst the people as the Holy Spirit desires. No one person has it all. No one person can fully function alone. We need each other for support, for love, for friendship, for accountability.

And finally, every aspect of the healing is touched by prayer. Prayer is an essential component of each step.

Prayer and relationship with God in every area in our lives is key, and therefore central in the diagram. It is almost a wheel within a wheel, to quote Ezekiel. It touches each aspect of our lives and healing program. It is intimately involved with each step, offering hope, faith, belief, friendship and encouragement along the way.

But what is this temple of God within us?

CHAPTER 3: THE TEMPLE OF GOD

I was amazed to find we are an exact replica of the city of God. Then I realized that man was created first. The city of Jerusalem was the replica. And if this is so, then it was given to show us something. It is the type and shadow of what is real.

I realize that it is the type and shadow of the city of New Jerusalem in the book of Revelation, but there is another application as it speaks to us here and now as well.

As I studied the map of ancient Jerusalem, I could see a human body in the form. Then, as I stared at the human re-creation of the city, I kept noticing the temple at the top of the neck. It was strategically placed in Jerusalem just as it is strategically placed within our body. It was placed right where the body connects to the skull. It was situated exactly where the brain stem connects to the spinal cord.

Then I began looking at what the temple really represents in the Bible.

It is where God sits on the Mercy Seat. It represented the presence of the Lord and the glory cloud (Exodus 13:21, 22, 40:33-38). It was where God communicated with Moses and the high priests. It was where God instructed the high priests about the things they needed to do for the people. It was also where the high priests talked to the Most High God.

It was the seat of communication between God and man.

The temple of God, the tabernacle of the Lord, the Holy of Holies is where the Lord communicates to His people.

Ephesians 4:13-16 tells us that Christ is the head and we are the body. I realize this is for the church as a whole, but if you were the only person saved then you would be the body and Christ would be your head. Let's make it just that simple.

We may no longer have the tabernacle in Jerusalem with the Ark of the Covenant, but we do have the Holy Spirit. Jesus sent the Holy Spirit to be with us after He left. Is it possible that the Holy Spirit actually resides in a certain spot in our body?

What is the work of the Holy Spirit? Could it be the same 11 things that are done at the gates of the city as shown in Chapter One?

1. He utters wisdom.
2. He teaches us right from wrong.
3. He redeems our bodies via deliverance and healing.
4. He proclaims who we are in Christ. He declares who the Father, Son and Holy Spirit are in us.
5. He teaches us Kingdom life.
6. He gives us gifts.
7. He seals us.

8. He gives us weapons of warfare: the belt of truth, the helmet of salvation, the shield of faith, the breastplate of righteousness, and the sword of the Spirit.
9. He purifies us with fire.
10. He teaches us righteousness and to love one another in unity.
11. He raises up the five-fold ministry to equip us: teachers, pastors, prophets, evangelists and apostles.

The Holy Spirit is sitting on the Mercy Seat of the temple we keep within us. But where is this Mercy Seat? And what is it?

Looking at the position of the temple in the drawings shown earlier, it is at the top of the neck. But what physically resides in this position?

There are over 206 bones in our bodies and they are all connected with a joint, a tendon or ligament. There is only 1 bone that is not connected to any others, in any way; joint, tendon or ligament. It is the Atlas or C1 vertebra of the spine.

The C1-Atlas is a bone that sits and rotates with the C2-Axis bone atop the spinal column. They are a unit together, working together to protect and house the brain stem and top of the nerve bundles of the spinal column.

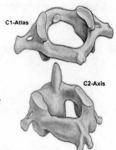

The first two vertebrae
of the spinal column

The Atlas sits on top of the Axis. It cradles the 8-14 pound skull which houses the brain. It allows the head to rotate while protecting the brain stem. One could almost say they were the Ark of the Covenant and the Mercy Seat.

Completely freeing one's imagination, you can almost see the top of the Mercy Seat in this bone. On either side of the Mercy Seat you can see the outstretched wings of the angels that guard the Mercy Seat. It has also been called the Mouth of God. Perhaps it is both.

You can see the two angels that sit at either end of the Mercy Seat and you can see where their wings join together as they cover the Mercy Seat. You can even see where the cloud of glory, the voice of God fits into the center of the C1-Atlas. It pinpoints the brain stem area.

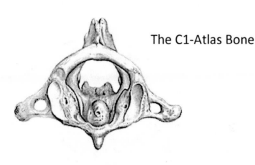

The C1-Atlas Bone

The two holes on the right and left sides of the Atlas accommodate two muscles. Unlike the other 31 vertebrae of the spinal column, these two vertebrae are designed specifically for rotation allowing for the wide range of motion of the neck.

Every aspect of body function is controlled by communication between the brain and the spinal cord which passes through the brain stem. The spinal cord is the main pathway for information connecting the brain to the peripheral nervous system. The spinal cord is divided into 31 segments which branches out to every part of the body.

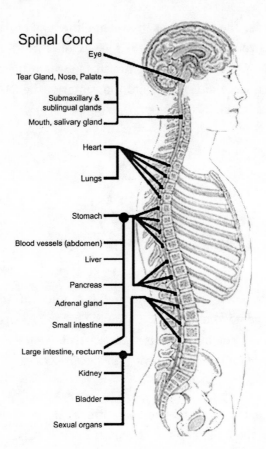

Spinal Cord

Eye

Tear Gland, Nose, Palate

Submaxillary &
sublingual glands

Mouth, salivary gland

Heart

Lungs

Stomach

Blood vessels (abdomen)

Liver

Pancreas

Adrenal gland

Small intestine

Large intestine, rectum

Kidney

Bladder

Sexual organs

Let's look at the numbers.

The atlas (C1) and axis (C2) are 2 special bones designed specifically for rotation. Two is the number of witness. God wants us to witness something here.

The C1-Atlas vertebra does not develop until the seventh

fetal month of the unborn child. Seven is indicative of completeness and fullness, once again showing that the completeness of man lies in the fullness of the Holy Spirit. Without the Holy Spirit, man is simply not complete. Salvation opens the door to learn Kingdom living, but it is the temple that gives the meaning of worship to the city.

The C1-Atlas and C2-Axis are crucial in allowing the communication to flow without interruption. If there is the slightest misalignment of these two bones, it begins to compress the brain stem. The brain stem communicates via 7 trillion nerves that continue down the spinal cord.

But let's look at the numbers again. Seven trillion is 1,000 x 1,000 x 1,000 x 7 which stands for the perfect fullness of the glory of God in divine completeness in Father, Son and Holy Spirit.

God has stamped His number and message even in the number of nerves in His body design.

These 7 trillion nerve endings control every aspect of our lives. We are to witness their work. And it is crucial for the well-being of the body to have that communication flow uninterrupted.

Just imagine, for one minute, if there is the slightest compression from a misalignment on just one hundred liver nerves... the liver will not function fully. It will not complete the task it was designed to accomplish, that is to cleanse the body of toxins. This applies to every system and activity that keeps us well.

What if it is the pancreas or adrenal glands or even the nerves that go to the knees or hands that are compressed even slightly? You can see that if any part of the seven trillion nerves is compressed this can cause problems. And as the years go by, the buildup of "no service zones" means that the messages for help from the body are not getting to the brain, and the messages to function/repair from the brain are not getting to the body.

Like the city of Jerusalem that was repaired in the day of Nehemiah, we were meant to be healed from the inside. The workmen lived in the city. The workmen worked on the walls from within the city. Just like Jerusalem, we have the ability to be healed from within our city if we allow the workmen to do their work.

The workers who repaired the city were slaves, kings and priests. They were goldsmiths and guards. They were every manner of people just as we have every manner of workers within us to do the work.

When the top vertebra is out of alignment, it will compress whatever bundle of nerves is in the way. With each person this compression may affect a different area of the body. As the years go by, and the compression remains uncorrected and worsens, the area affected will slip from distress into disease.

Some of the diseases that have been helped by readjusting the alignment of this C1-Atlas bone are:

allergies

arm pain

arthritis

asthma

athletic injuries

Attention Deficit Disorder

back pain

bed wetting

Carpal Tunnel Syndrome

Cerebral Palsy

Child Development Problems

chronic infection

constipation

depression

digestive problems

ear infections

epileptic seizures

eye infections

female disorders

fever

flu symptoms

frequent colds

hacking cough

hay fever

headaches (all types)

herniated disc

high blood pressure

hip pain

hyperactivity

Immune System Deficiency

indigestion

infertility

knee pain

learning disability

leg pain

loss of sleep

low back pain

Menieres Disease

migraines

multiple sclerosis

muscle spasms

neck pain

nervousness

neuralgia

neuritis

pain (chronic)

poor vision

restlessness

Scoliosis

shoulder pain

sore throat

T.M.J. Syndrome

Tendinitis

tight muscles

tingling sensations

Tinnitus

Tourrette Syndrome

whiplash

In order for the temple to be repaired within us, we must, as the Levites, tend to the temple. We are the temple of the Holy Spirit and so we must pay attention to its maintenance.

First we must spend time with the Lord. We must build the relationship just like we would build our marital relationships. We are the Bride of Christ, the sons and daughters of the Father and the temple of the Holy Spirit. There are three members of the Godhead. There must be three relationships, one with each of them, to be an undefiled bride and child.

To become that undefiled bride we must heal in a bath of myrrh. Regardless of what our lives have been, it is not the life God designed for us. It has involved stress, oppression, fear, traumas, etc., and these, regardless of how large or small, have to be healed. Scars may remain, but the festering wounds must be healed if we are to move into kingdom living.

Next we must take out the garbage that was in the city. The Dung Gate was repaired because it was essential to get the garbage out of the city to the pit outside the walls. Remember we are that city needing to be cleansed. We need to deliver the garbage to the pit outside the walls.

Next, we need to allow the mouth of God to open, putting the Mercy Seat straight upon the Ark of Covenant. We need to open that communication between the head (Christ) and the body, us (church). There can be no disruption of flow.

Like the attending Levites, there must be movement within

the temple. Everything within the Temple needs to be cleansed and maintained. This requires exercise, not only physical, but emotional and spiritual as well. We need to exercise the body as much as we need to exercise our faith.

Next, it is essential to properly nourish the body for efficient repairs, growth and function. This does not mean a steady diet of dead convenience foods that retain no nutrition. It means looking after our bodies as God intended with fresh, live fruits, vegetables, seeds and grains. Live bodies require live food. We must eat whole foods to provide the required nutritional components.

Next, we need to be in community with others. We were not created to be alone. We need each other. We must work together. This was of such importance to Jesus, that it was one of the few recorded prayers spoken by Jesus. You will find it in John 17:6-19. We were created to be in community one with another, to be one as the Godhead is one.

Finally, a strong, faithful prayer life with the Father, the Son and the Holy Spirit develops relationship. They are not interested in pre-programmed prayers but in heart-to-heart communication, between friends. We are to be the Bride of Christ. He is our Husband. Should we not talk to Him as wife? We are co-laborers and helpmates. We need to improve our communication skills to line up each area of our life with His will. He is not only interested but intimately involved in our lives. This is our eight-step program to restoration and health.

CHAPTER 4: MY JOURNEY

It has been a life-long journey for me to arrive at the understanding I have now. Many puzzle pieces have slowly come together. The eight-step program has progressively developed through trial and error with successes gained along the way.

The eight-step program reflects the process we have learned through successes in both my life and the lives of many of my friends to regain our lives.

Restoring communication with the Lord was not as easy as it sounds. There is a tendency with each one of us to concentrate on one of the Godhead and forget the others. There are those who are "drunk" in the Spirit but who forget to read the word or develop any depth with the Father and Son. There are those who love Jesus but forget the Holy Spirit and Father exist with as much reality as their true love. There are those who pay attention only to the Father to the exclusion of a relationship with their savior who died for them or the Holy Spirit who teaches them.

It is not an easy thing to build a relationship with all three of the Godhead with equal passion and love as we have felt for the main focus of our attention. It takes a concerted effort at first, but the rewards are immeasurable.

This was my first task—to realize that the Godhead is three individual personages who require my attention, affection and love.

I read the word and discovered that each one played a different role in the lives of Their people. Each one had a different responsibility which meant that each one was to be approached within their specified areas.

This liberated me from things I had been taught that simply locked up my relationship with the Lord. I learned to let each one be who they were instead of trying to fit them all into a mold. I let each one of them out of the box of my limitations and allowed them to be who they are.

I discovered this was the easy part when the time came to face my personal emotional healing. I had to forgive so many people who had hurt me. The list was very long indeed. Words spoken over me, curses shouted out, things done to me... all had to be forgiven and released. Things as seemingly insignificant as being cut off in traffic cause a trauma that loom as an open door for offence and fear.

Injuries were heaped upon a fragile, childlike faith—a faith crushed and shattered while very young, and yet it too had to be forgiven. Abuses were inflicted by those who held power over me. Some abusers were family, some were authority figures in school or at work. All of these people had to be forgiven. I had to let go of all the wounds, offenses, intimidations...and of course, many of these situations led to fears and more fears, as well as anger, resentment, etc. Everything had to go if I wanted to be healed. I had to learn to sit in that bath of myrrh with patience and tolerance for as long as it took for forgotten things to be washed away. Sometimes I had help. Sometimes I was alone. Always I was under the watchful eye of a loving God who stayed with me every step of the way.

We have all learned a great deal of negativity (fear) in our lives and we have to replace each instance with the positive (hope) love of God for us. We have to replace the lies we have been led to believe with the truth that is foreign to our ears.

But breaking the traumas and closing the open wounds, and letting the wounds and injuries heal is not enough. We have to get rid of the pus that keeps festering within the wound. We might not be able to do anything about the cause of the injury, but we can clean out the pus that keeps the wound from healing.

I entered a period of deliverance. For this I developed a very simple guideline. We are created in the image of God. We were designed to follow the plumb line of the Father's own nature—one of love, patience, tolerance, peace.

Since that is how I was created, everything that is not the Father's nature—hate, jealousy, bitterness, wrath, despair, fear, depression—are activated by spirits. Everything that is not of God, is quite simply, the devil. There is no other reality.

When I recognize an incident has occurred to reopen an old wound—words of rejection, or hurtful words spoken—I forgive the speaker, I ask the Lord to heal the wound but often find it still festers. That is when I know there is a spirit pushing that button. Get rid of the spirit and the festering pus is gone. I have been delivered of a great many spirits since I inherited an unusual number of them from my generational lines.

I realize that much more depth is required on this topic, but deliverance is not the primary purpose for this book. If you would like to find further information on how to be free from your unseen tormentors visit http://www.aftapm.com (Ask For The Ancient Paths Ministry)

Most people who are Christians believe they cannot be possessed by a spirit. But they forget that Jesus came to His own people, the Jews, to deliver, heal and to teach. It was His own chosen people, the people of God, who He ministered to, because they were in need, just as we are in need.

We are that people. It is for our sins, disease and spiritual affliction by fallen angels that He died. He died so we could be restored. Romans 7 and 8 teach us that even Paul, the greatest apostle of New Testament times, was plagued with the man of sin that dwelt within. He did what he did not want to do and did not do what he wanted to do because of that man of sin he battled with; the fallen nature we have inherited.

We need to be delivered of the very things that keep us bound to the past and to the enemy. This leg of my journey has taken 10 years and still continues on as the Lord shows me new things in my life that need to be discarded. This does not make me any less of a Christian, just a cleaner one than many. It is not because I am special, just obedient. If I want to have the whole life He has given me, then I must chose to follow the path the Lord has set out for us.

I quickly realized that the next step to health was to get the Upper Cervical vertebra in alignment. It was obvious to me that my premature birth played a huge part in my current condition since the atlas bone is not fully developed by the seventh month. So, of course my 7th month C-Section delivery only added to the trauma placed on my incomplete Upper Cervical vertebra due to the abrupt process of birth. At this point my little C1-Atlas was terribly misaligned.

Add to this the usual childhood head injuries and falls, I knew that it was definitely related to most of my physical ills.

I was being healed and delivered, but soon realized that all my efforts to change nutritional and exercise habits without having this vital bone realigned would not achieve the results I desired. It would take a combined effort on all fronts to regain my health and have my city repaired or even rebuilt.

I excitedly made an appointment for my first correction. I have been to medical doctors for 56 years and chiropractors regularly for well over 30 years. But I knew this time would be different.

I can tell you the very minute the noise began in my ear. Sometimes it is deafening, so I raise my voice so I can hear myself speak. I was 18 years old, lying on my stomach in bed listening to Cher singing Half-breed. Yes, it was that long ago. I took an aspirin. It was around noon.

It is interesting the number 18 stands for bondage. I plunged into hearing bondage that sometimes was so intense I thought I would go crazy with the noise.

The noise began and has remained at varying levels of deafening distraction for 38 years (again, slavery). I was enslaved to that noise. It stole my sleep, my waking hours, my ability to hear the voices of my friends.

But after my first alignment, suddenly the silence was deafening. It was gone! It was gone for the first time in 38 years. It lasted for four hours before it slowly returned to a lesser degree. It no longer is louder than life around me. It has become simply background noise I sometimes do not hear at all.

Every day of my 56 years of life has existed with pain. But I was suddenly pain-free for the first time...for an entire two hours before it too slowly returned to a lesser degree.

In short, I kept my correction for four hours. That, I was told, was the "shock factor." But I had a taste of promised hope and wellness. After that initial feeling, my body began to do all sorts of odd things. It felt as if things were actually shifting around. It is called the "healing factor" or "crisis factor."

The restored relationship with the Lord, inner healing, and deliverance allowed me not only to accept the correction but to keep it without a great deal of effort. They all played an important role to this vital correction. It is not to say my body would otherwise not have accepted the correction and be healed, but it does mean that things have progressed at a much more rapid pace.

With the Upper Cervical correction, my brain stem was no longer compressed and so the messages to and from my brain and body were now able to be sent and delivered unhindered. Things were beginning to work properly, according to design.

Exercise and nutritional food have never been my high priority. I lived a sedentary lifestyle giving little thought to what I ate provided I liked it and little or no preparation effort was involved. This had to change if I was to get well. I had to concentrate on walking every day or at least several times a week. And my diet changed from frozen foods or preferably restaurants to mostly raw foods as I determined to become a vegetarian.

The lifestyles changes I was making were drastic but necessary. I have never felt better or healthier...and I have only just begun.

So let's look at the eight-step program in more detail.

CHAPTER 5. RELATIONSHIP WITH THE GODHEAD

In Genesis 1:26 we have our first introduction to God being in fact three Gods in one. The Hebrews' cry of, "Hear, O Israel, the Lord our God, the LORD is one!" (Deuteronomy 6:4) rings true. There is only one God...but He is 3. They are the Father, the Son and the Holy Spirit. We need to develop an independent relationship with each individually.

There are so many explanations instructing one how to get close to God, but they all lack one thing—honesty. We build a relationship with God the same way we build a relationship with a spouse, a parent or a friend. We tell the truth.

This is a difficult concept for most people because we expend such effort trying to appear as we think appropriate, instead of being real. Honesty is the very way to salvation.

Lord Jesus I have been in control of my life and I have made a mess of it. It is empty without you. I accept your perfect sacrifice that you have died to pay the price of my rebellion. I repent of my sins, the things I have done against you, others or myself, and I ask for your forgiveness. I apply the precious blood of Jesus to my life and ask that you clean away all that was filthy rags and clothe me with the righteousness of your salvation. In Jesus' name, amen.

With hat in hand, we declare in all honesty we have made a mess of our lives. God's way has got to be better than our way. It is a simple, honest realization. It is a simple, honest statement.

It is the honesty that gets us back on track. It is the honesty that reaches across the breach and begins the restoration of relationship. It is only the honesty that will maintain any relationship, allowing it to deepen and flourish.

What kind of a relationship can you have with your spouse without honesty? Is this a key to the divorce rate now soaring past 50 percent? We enter relationships dishonestly, whether through fear of not being accepted or just deception, and it follows throughout the relationship like a threatening shadow. It will bring mistrust, anger, betrayal and disappointment. Not to mention the destructive effects on the children; rejection, guilt, anger, fear....

This is the same struggle most people have with their relationship with the Lord—keeping it real. We very quickly opt out of the initial honest, open relationship to empty prayers that are simply "Gimme! Gimme! Gimme!" shopping lists. We might assuage the guilt of our endless lists of requests by adding a few things for other people. But it is just as artificial, the same pretense that ends in divorce.

I counsel people to do things with the Lord. Take Him shopping with you. Ask His opinion about a dress or a pair of jeans. Take Him fishing. Invite Him out for a drive or a walk. Tell Him what a great job He did on that flowering tree, or beautiful rose bush that has suddenly delighted you today. Tell Him what an exceptional gift the sunrise was to you this morning. "I so appreciate Your work."

I have often asked, while on a road trip, to see something I would not normally see. I especially like to see buffalo slowly regaining in numbers. He has never disappointed me. Once a herd of deer jumped across the Trans-Canada Highway on a beautiful afternoon. He has brought coyotes, wolves, mountain sheep, hawks, eagles, bears, etc. across my path over the years. He has never disappointed me because I delight and take joy in what He has created.

We miss the importance of our call, which is the reason we were created. Rather than the usual thoughts regarding why we were created, I am going straight to Song of Solomon, too often an overlooked book. We were created to be the helpmate of Jesus, our husband. We are created to be the Bride of Christ.

Most people enjoy the image of how wonderful it will be to rule and reign with the King of the universe while missing the point altogether. It isn't about our power, but His. We were created to be cared for by the King of creation, to run by His side and enjoy everything He has created for us. We were created to enjoy His creation. I am His creation, you are His creation. He did it all for our enjoyment.

Simply, we were created to enjoy life, the life He has given us in abundance. He is a God of abundance, a God of increase, a God of all things good. He has created everything that ever was, is and will be and He has created everything for us to enjoy.

We will spend eternity not playing a harp on some cloud, but in building relationships with angels, with every other person who chose the Father of truth.

What a concept! We will live in eternity giving and loving instead of taking and hating. No more conglomerates or big business. No more starvation, want or lack. No more deception, lies, loss or theft. No more taxes, penalties or fines. No more negative.

We will eat our own bread and wear our own clothes. There will be no locks on the doors of our houses or on the doors of our hearts. We will be in relationship with God the Father, God the Son, God the Holy Spirit and with each other.

The Father supplies all our needs. It is from Him that all life began and came into existence. It is from Him that all life and everything that has been created had its origin and conception. He is the One who is anxious to forgive and hold us safely in His arms. He is the One who cannot do enough for us, who is long in patience and great in love. He is the One who waits a lifetime to hear the words—"our Father…."

The Son is the Word. He spoke the command for all things that have been created to be created. He gave His life for the very creation that despised Him and crucified Him (don't be too sure that you would not have been in the crowd calling for His life. I know I would have been). He died so you and I would have an opportunity to restore the relationship we and our forefathers tossed away so callously. He died so we could live. And He rose again so we would find the way to eternal life through Him. He is the one who is willing to cover our nakedness instantly with His righteousness, just for the asking. He is the one who is quick to cover our sins with His own blood, just for the asking. He is the one who is there the instant we come to Him and repent of wanting our own way, a way that does not work. He is the one who seeks after us, wooing us, our entire life to restore us to the relationship that has been severed with the Godhead, desiring that we return to Him before it is too late. Return before death takes away our last opportunity for salvation.

The Holy Spirit is the one responsible for actually creating everything the Father thought and the Son spoke. He is the Doer. He is the One who teaches and leads. He is the Comforter. He is the One who wipes our tears. He is the One who lives within us and stays with us through thick and thin, teaching us in the ways of righteousness with gentle promptings. He will give us directions while we are driving. He will help us with life decisions, pointing out the better way in every situation. How often I wished I had listened to that quiet voice within instead of my own way. How many times have you said, too late, "I knew that" He was there, faithfully. We did not listen.

We need to build that relationship with all three of the Godhead; Father, Son and Holy Spirit. We do that by spending time with each one of them; when walking, driving, exercising, a coffee break, or simply quiet time especially for them like reading the Bible or listening to worship.

Include them in your life as you would your spouse, parents, siblings or friends. Include them in every aspect of your life. There is no place or situation that does not interest or concern Them because They created you. They want to be involved in your life. Why? Because They want you to share your special and unique outlook and appreciation of life with Them.

You are unique and you have a unique perspective on life. They want to share with you that unique perspective of the life and creation They have made.

It is like sharing life with your child as they discover new things—it brings an entirely new appreciation for life to your heart. It is like sharing life with a lover—it brings out an entirely new excitement for your life to your heart.

Who does not remember the first picture that your child made with the paper and crayons you supplied? It was a marvel to see them create with the tools you provided. They took what you provided and added their own creative life. That is what we bring to the table and that delights the Lord.

We are created in His likeness—He is creative, so we are creative. We are made to give that creativity away in love, peace and joy. What a calling we have on our lives, to be like the King of Kings. To be His queen. To be His child. To be His love. To be the apple of His eye. To let Him think of us 24/7. To let Him desire us all day and night for all eternity.

What an inheritance. We are called to live eternity being in relationship with the God who created everything and enjoy everything He has created. What are you waiting for? Many are held back because of fear.

This is the fear of being honest, or of exposure. And yet, that is the only place we can begin and the only way we can remain in relationship with God or anyone else. It is even the only way we can be in relationship with ourselves. Take a chance. He is trustworthy... and waiting to welcome you.

CHAPTER 6: INNER HEALING AND DELIVERANCE

Revelation 22:2 "Between the main street and the river was the Tree of Life producing twelve kinds of fruit, a different kind every month; and the leaves of the tree were for the healing of the nations." (CJB)

It is interesting that Jesus healed all kinds of sickness and disease among the people (Matthew 4:23). He went among His own people to heal them. We are those people.

But why are there 12 fruits for 12 months?

The number 12 stands for governmental rule of the king and queen. Interesting how this number parallels the book of Esther. Esther had to spend 6 months healing in a bath of myrrh. The number 6 stands for the number of man, the weakness of man and the inventions of man. Then she spent 6 months learning Kingdom living.

Because there are 2 separate 6-month time periods, I am suggesting that the first 6 months were for healing from the weakness of man, while the latter were healing from the inventions of man by learning Kingdom living... learning the ways of God after being cleansed of a soiled life.

What are the 12 things from which we need to be healed? I believe the clue is in the 12 tribes of Israel.

In Revelation 7:5-8, the list of the 12 tribes are:

1. Judah: He shall be praised
2. Reuben: behold a son
3. Gad: a troop
4. Asher: blessed
5. Naphtali: wrestling
6. Manasseh: forgetting
7. Simeon: hearkening
8. Levi: joined
9. Issachar: man of hire, reward
10. Zebulun: a habitation
11. Joseph: let him add
12. Benjamin: son of the right hand; son of good fortune

Judah: We shall be healed of that which plagues the meaning of Judah. The opposite of *praise* is condemnation and depreciation. It is a complainer who bears false witness and condemns or depreciates someone else's worth. The first thing to be healed is a complaining heart because of perceived lack.

Reuben: We shall be healed of that which plagues the meaning of Reuben. The opposite of *behold a son* is rejection and abandonment, a breach in relationship. The second thing to be healed is a restoration of family relationships. We will become part of a family as God brings brothers and sisters, mothers and fathers into our lives in abundance.

Gad: We shall be healed of that which plagues the meaning of Gad. The opposite of *a troop* is being alone, loneliness. It seems to be the human condition to feel separated and alone. That void will be filled not only with one other, but a troop. We will become part of a group—the body of Christ.

Asher: We shall be healed of that which plagues the meaning of Asher. The opposite of *blessed* is cursed. We have been cursed because of the sin of Eve and Adam. We have lived under a curse, but we shall be blessed. We shall move out from under the curse and be healed of the effects of the curse and shall be healed and blessed.

Naphtali: We shall be healed of that which plagues the meaning of Naphtali. The meaning of Naphtali is wrestling. It doesn't seem to be much of a blessing until we look at the story of Jacob who wrestled with the Lord for a blessing. The Lord asked him specifically to reveal his name which meant *supplanter*. And He replaced Jacob's name with a new name, Israel. Israel means *God prevails*. We will be healed of wrestling with ourselves to determine who will be in control of our life. We will be healed of trying to supplant the One who created us and is rightfully our God through creation, redemption and adoption. God will prevail in our lives and we shall finally be at peace.

Manasseh: We shall be healed of that which plagues the meaning of Manasseh. We will no longer remember the past; the hurts, the abuses, the wounds and the crushing. We will forget. Our tears shall be wiped away and we will forget the pain, embracing joy, peace and life instead of hanging on to memories that cause strife, stealing our joy and bringing death.

Simeon: We shall learn the rules of Kingdom life. We shall hearken to the voice of the King and be healed of not listening, of not paying attention.

Levi: We shall be joined to the King, as Esther was joined to the King. We shall no longer be an island. We shall be joined not only to the King but to the people of the Kingdom, accepting responsibility for each other. We shall be healed of not caring, of being unloving.

Issachar: We shall learn the rules of Kingdom life for we will no longer be a servant, a man of hire. We shall have the reward of being adopted into the house of Royalty as the Bride of the Son, Bride of the King. We shall be healed of our slavery and servitude as we are adopted into the Royal Family of God.

Zebulun: We shall learn the rules of Kingdom life, never again empty. For we will be healed of not having a purpose. We shall be the habitation of the King. We shall never be empty or alone again.

Joseph: We shall learn the rules of Kingdom life and turn aside from the lack that has besieged us. For Kingdom life is a life of abundance and addition. We shall be healed of all poverty and lack as we walk into prosperity and fullness.

Benjamin: We shall learn the rules of Kingdom life, no longer the son who cleans out the swine trough for food, but we become the son of the right hand, son of good fortune. We are healed of destitution and despair as we learn who we are in Christ and who we were created to be.

Healing takes time, and as Esther, she had to sit quietly in a bath of myrrh, tended by those who minister to us and serve us. She had to be still, letting the healing power of the myrrh soak in before she was prepared to learn the rules of Kingdom life. Then she had to turn away from everything she had known, in order to learn a completely different concept, a new way to live.

We must take that time, to sit both in the bath and at the feet of the teacher—the Holy Spirit.

Jesus brought deliverance to His people. Everywhere He went He healed sickness and disease, and delivered the oppressed. He did not deliver or heal the outsider. He healed and delivered His own people.

We are that people. The Old and New Testament are filled

with references of spirits that cause diseases in God's people. In fact, Deuteronomy 28 outlines exactly what brings on the curse of the enemy, which is sickness, disease, poverty, barrenness and death. Romans 8 tells us of the problem Paul had, doing the things he did not want to do and not able to do the things he wanted to do. It was because the man of sin lived within him.

Christians need to appropriate the blood of Christ into every aspect of their lives. This includes appropriating His deliverance for our lives in every corner we find the enemy lurking - hiding in the bushes. The spirits of anger, bitterness, antichrist, fear, etc. are some of the names of those enemies. You can find a list of them at http://www.aftapm.com. "When in doubt, cast them out," is my motto.

As the children of Israel took possession of the Promised Land, the Lord promised to go before them chasing the enemy out of the bushes with hornets. That is the job of the Holy Spirit. But it was the children of Israel who still had to get them out of the land. The Holy Spirit will tell us where the problem lies, but we are still responsible to do the work...to evict the unwanted tenant.

Jesus died to give us the keys to the kingdom. One of these keys is deliverance. It is in the authority of Jesus and His sacrifice and by the blood that He shed that we can be freed of every enemy in our land. The more we become free, the more the Holy Spirit can inhabit, the more of the temple (our bodies) God can inhabit.

Every trauma that is experienced in life—a startling loud noise or sudden fright, an accident, a fall, a traffic incident, a domestic trial etc. all potentially open the door for a spirit to enter into our beings. Fear, stress and anxiety are the favorites of traumas, but there is also hatred, anger, bitterness, jealousy, etc. We simply need to place that trauma under the blood of Jesus to close the door; forgive who needs to be forgiven even if it is ourselves, or even God because we perceived that He wasn't there for us; repent of allowing that spirit to work in our lives; and finally, cast out the demon in the name of Jesus by the power of His blood that was shed for our freedom.

Jesus went to His people to show them freedom, then He ultimately gave His life to provide for that freedom because He was innocent of any sin. We need only to accept His offer of freedom and get the enemy out of our land.

Doing the spiritual healing simultaneously with the physical healing will increase and speed the physical healing due to the freedom gained from the hold of the enemy. The spiritual world came first so our spiritual healing comes first. Then God created the physical world with all its wonders. The wonder of physical healing comes next.

CHAPTER 7. UPPER CERVICAL CHIROPRACTIC

When any part of the body is in distress, the brain sends the appropriate messages to initiate healing into the affected area. The brain is command central with the control to activate whatever process is required to repair the problem. But it can only do this if there is an open channel of communication between the brain and body via the nerves that connect to the brain stem.

When those repair messages are blocked, the progression of distress will continue until eventually deteriorating into disease.

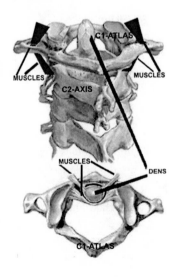

This is a diagram of the top of the spinal cord. The C1 is attached via several muscles allowing it to pivot and rotate so the head moves freely. The Dens of the C2 is held into place with muscles allowing the neck to rotate.

When the C1-Atlas is out of alignment, it puts stress on the muscles that hold it in place. These muscles will cause the body to misalign in order to compensate. It is the body's primary mission to keep the head on straight. If it is slightly misaligned, certain muscles will tighten up attempting to compensate, causing other joints to misalign, creating pain, arthritis and spurs.

I was so disappointed to see the spurs in my neck that had developed over the years because they are irreversible. Earlier treatments of Upper Cervical corrections would have reduced or avoided the problem altogether. The spurs were created by the pressure, rubbing and stress of misaligned vertebrae resulting in the formation of additional bone on the vertebrae.

This is what the C1-Atlas should look like – the skull and vertebrae sitting straight with an unimpaired flow of information from the brain/body to the brain/body.

Based on the drawings of Daniel O. Day.

The C1-Atlas is misaligned, impeding the flow of information from the brain to the body. The muscles are tensed on the left side while the muscles on the right side are stretched to accommodate the misalignment.

Brain messages control, maintain and monitor all aspects of body functions. When the body is in distress anywhere, these messages also dispatch healing. When messages are blocked because of nerve compression at the brain stem, malfunctions will result. Any system allowed to malfunction, will eventually deteriorate into disease and degeneration. Consider how dependable your vehicle would be if you continually ignored the warning lights demanding attention. Imagine driving into a wall, totally misaligning the axle, then trying to drive on an angle! Your body's Atlas is your axle.

However, there are specialists who gently remedy this situation alleviating the compression. They are called Upper Cervical Chiropractic Doctors and they specialize in realigning the C1-Atlas and C2-Axis of the spinal column.

The primary purpose of UCC doctors in this specialized field is to re-position the weight of the head directly over the center of the neck. This removes spinal cord compression and restores body alignment. By alleviating spinal cord compression, the flow of messages from the brain to the affected parts of the body is reactivated, allowing the natural healing process to begin.

As shown on the previous page, the spinal column remains in alignment as long as the 8-14 pound weight of the head remains centered on the Atlas. However, if the weight of the head is not balanced directly over the brain stem, nerve compression will result.

The body automatically compensates for any misalignment by tilting in the opposite direction. The eyes will always seek to level with the horizon. It is called the Righting Reflex. Maintaining a level eye line may mean the head is straight, but if the Atlas is not level, everything else will shift to maintain balance. One shoulder raised, the spine is now twisted, and the pelvis is no longer level effectively shortening one leg, and weakening the overstretched muscles...and so begins the breakdown of communication.

Millions of messages are transmitted per second back and forth between the brain and body. These messages send updates of malfunction from the body's operating systems to the brain and responding messages of restoration and healing from the brain to maintain the body. If the brain does not pick up the call, it cannot send the method of rescue to induce healing. No healing instruction received means the distress increases, multiplying into pain or breakdown into disease.

These messages control every organ and system which operates the body: circulation, respiration, digestion, elimination, nervous system, and the critical glandular/ hormonal endocrine system which controls chemical responses and balance on a continual basis. These messages maintain the optimum working order of every cell to keep us in health. A problem in the communication center which is the brain stem will delete necessary updates. If there is the slightest bit of compression something in the body suffers and will eventually atrophy into ill health.

The long-term effect is degeneration in the part of the body that is served by the restricted nerves. This degeneration causes pain, lowers the resistance to illness and can affect organ function, eventually leading to disease, and/or loss of mobility in limbs and joints.

Body imbalance or C1-Atlas misalignment occurs well before pain begins.

Body imbalance or C1-Atlas misalignment is noticeable in a number of different ways. It can be a head tilt, restricted neck movement, one shoulder lower than another, abnormal spinal curvature, one hip higher than another, one leg shorter than another, bilateral body weight difference, or even bilateral temperature variations.

It is something most of us experience so regularly we have come to disregard the signs. However, it is something that is both crucial to a healthy lifestyle and easily corrected.

Body imbalance or C1-Atlas misalignment is restored and corrected by an Upper Cervical spinal correction.

A short physical examination and a series of x-rays is all that is required to determine the extent of the C1-Atlas misalignment. The x-rays are studied to determine the precise degree of correction required to put the C1-Atlas back into alignment by a painless instrument or hand correction.

The Upper Cervical procedure will simply free your body to heal itself by removing the spinal cord compression which releases the brain's transmission of neuron messages to the affected part of the body.

As soon as the spinal correction is made the body balance will begin to be restored. Immediately muscles begin to relax, blood and oxygen circulation is increased and healing messages are transmitted throughout the body.

It is not unusual to experience a variety of changes in your body after the correction as a result of the body responding to this structural correction. The body must go through different cycles of repair which may present in a variety of ways:

- cold-like symptoms such as nasal mucous discharge as the body goes through a cleansing process
- light-headedness
- possible slight headache
- alleviation of pain
- alleviation of symptoms
- tingling or heat sensations
- muscle stiffness or weakness as you adapt to this realignment
- pain in the area of an old injury
- body elimination changes such as diarrhea or constipation

The severity of the condition determines the recovery time. The healing process does take some time.

The first objective will be to restore the body's alignment, thus reactivating the self-healing process. The first six to eight weeks after a C1-Atlas correction are considered to be a stabilization and healing period. The balancing and stabilizing of the spine takes time.

You should be prepared to maintain the balance of your body with regular checkups to make sure there is no brain stem or nerve compression, i.e., your correction is holding.

It is recommended that you do not sleep on your stomach as this twists the neck. This was one of the hardest things for me to change. You should also avoid using your head to raise or turn your body. You should never cradle your phone between your head and your shoulder. You should also avoid reaching or straining. And finally, you should avoid twisting and turning your head too far, rolling your head or tilting it too far back. This can cause you to lose your correction while the muscles are retraining and strengthening.

It is vital that proper balance be maintained between your brain stem and your spinal cord in order to receive benefits from all the other efforts you are making to maintain your temple.

For more information on Upper Cervical Chiropractic, please see the following websites.

1. International Christian Servants
   http://www.icservants.org/
2. http://UpperCervicalAdvocates.com/
3. http://www.Upcspine.com
4. http://www.GetWellGetHealthy.com
5. http://www.UPCSPINE.com
6. http://www.NUCCA.org
7. http://www.Orthospinology.org
8. http://www.KCUCS.org
9. http://www.UCHCA.com
10. http://www.Blair.com
11. http://www.advancedorthogonal.com
12. http://www.uppercervicaldoctors.com

<u>Please note:</u> If you are interested in seeking an Upper Cervical Spinal Correction, you need to see a qualified Upper Cervical Chiropractic Doctor to receive a proper correction. An Upper Cervical Spinal Correction is not the same thing as a Rotary Break.

If you suspect your upper cervical area is not positioned properly, please consult an Upper Cervical Chiropractic Doctor who has specialized training in this area. UC DC's will use one or more of these special techniques to analyze, correct and monitor the upper cervical area. Corrective procedures and techniques of this critical area require proper education and experience. This book is NOT written to discredit Chiropractors in any way; it is simply to discuss the different approach of the specialty techniques of the upper cervical area.

CHAPTER 8: EXERCISE AND NUTRITION

There is a growing interest in exercise. Physical exercise strengthens the muscles and cardiovascular system, encourages weight loss by burning calories, boosts the immune system, improves mental health, helps prevent depression, and helps prevent certain diseases.

Physical exercise also contributes to maintaining healthy bone density, muscle strength and joint mobility. Exercise reduces levels of cortisol, a stress hormone that builds fat in the abdominal region.

Aerobic exercise has been shown to reduce serious chronic conditions such as high blood pressure, heart disease, Type 2 diabetes, insomnia and depression.

There is no doubt that exercise is an important part of life, but it has almost become an obsession in today's society in a desperate attempt to maintain youth. However, too much exercise can be harmful. The body needs a day of rest which is why so many health experts suggest that you exercise every other day. Inappropriate exercise can be harmful...the term "inappropriate" will vary between individuals. Unaccustomed overexertion of muscles leads to damage of the muscle and joints. In females, excessive exercise can cause unhealthy menstrual changes.

Movement is essential for optimum health. God gave us muscles for working but anything in excess can be destructive. The most natural exercise is walking, running, swimming, biking, sports...things that do not demand over achievement.

Proper nutrition is even more important to optimum health. Proper nutrition is essential to provide the body with building blocks for both growth and healing, and for normal maintenance. But what is proper nutrition?

I will only touch on the science of proper diet because there is ample information available, but I will go into Biblical references in answer to one important question. What were we initially created to eat?

In Genesis, man was given fruits, vegetables, seeds, beans, grains and nuts. Man was made to be an herbivore, not a carnivore. This is evident by the various characteristics or differences between a carnivore and an herbivore.

Unlike a carnivore's teeth, our teeth are not pointed but are flat edged for biting, crushing and grinding. Our jaws cannot rip flesh from flesh, but move side-to-side and back-to-front, motions which are excellent for crushing and grinding grains and high fiber foods. Unlike a carnivore's saliva, which does not contain digestive enzymes, our saliva contains alkaline carbohydrate digestive enzymes.

Animal flesh requires an excessive amount of uric acid to break down its complex protein. A carnivore liver is capable of eliminating 10 times more uric acid than a human liver. Obviously the carnivore is designed to digest animal protein, we are not. Uric acid is a toxic chemical that needs to be flushed from the body, if not fully eliminated the kidneys may form crystals which develop into stones.

Man must cook his meat in order to destroy E. Coli bacteria, salmonella, parasites or other pathogens that would not survive in the stomach of a carnivore. To avoid adverse pathogens, a carnivore has roughly 10 times the amount of hydrochloric acid than a human stomach.

Carnivores eliminate quickly rotting flesh from their intestines through a very short digestive system, ¼ the length of a human intestine. Unlike man's colon, a carnivore's colon is short, straight and smooth in order to quickly eliminate fatty wastes high in cholesterol before they have a chance to putrefy.

Genesis 1:29-30 tells us that we were designed to eat every herb, seed, fruit, vegetable, and nut. We were designed to be herbivores.

Meat was given to man to eat after the fall of Adam and Eve through sin. Eating flesh spreads or breeds the condition of sin, sickness and death in our lives.

The optimum diet should consist of 70% raw foods to give us the full range of nutrient and enzymes. Raw foods help the body heal from the cellular level.

Raw foods are alive. Cooked, processed foods with synthetic vitamins, preservatives, and additives are dead. The lab cannot differentiate between dead and live nutrients, hence either is promoted acceptable. However the critical difference between raw and cooked is the change in pH. A substantial increase in acidity not only makes the food unusable but harmful to the optimum pH balance at which our bodies function. Search out which foods are alkaline and include as many as possible into your diet.

There are so many benefits to eating raw foods. A raw alkaline diet including lots of water will reduce fat cells which were formed to act as a protective storage unit for the harmful acid and chemical intake which has overtaken our food source. Our body is constantly attempting to heal the damage we inflict on ourselves. So give yourself a break and investigate a better diet.

Raw foods are rich in antioxidants, water and phyto-nutrients, providing all the nutrients our bodies need for optimal health. In fact, an all-plant raw diet provides all the essential amino acids (proteins) and nutrients to meet our body's nutritional needs (U.S. Department of Agriculture; U.S. Department of Health Services). The World Health Organization states that we need only 5% of the calories we eat to come from protein.

The current recommendation is that our dietary protein needs are only .08-1.2 grams for every 2.2 pounds under normal circumstances. We can find protein in nuts, seeds, dark, leafy green vegetables, fruits, sprouted grains and sprouted legumes. And protein from raw foods is readily digestible which means it does not sit in your stomach feeling heavy i.e. rotting, till removed.

Calcium also can be found in nuts, vegetables, seeds, sprouted grains, fruits and sea vegetables. In fact, iron and all essential vitamins, minerals and nutrients can be found in abundance in raw foods, without the heat of cooking that destroy so much of the nutrients essential for our well-being.

I would like to add just a quick word about water. HYDRATE HYDRATE HYDRATE. Because so many of our beverage choices are acidic, even the water, our bodies are not getting oxygenated. Ever notice those really expensive bottled waters are alkaline? Try adding a pinch of baking soda to your glass and drink much more water.

"We are what we eat," is a very accurate statement that should be considered when embracing wellness. We were created to continually heal while our cells are made to reproduce and replace themselves.

And we must never forget that everything in life moves...and so should we.

CHAPTER 9: COMMUNITY

"All mankind is of one author, and is one volume; when one man dies, one chapter is not torn out of the book, but translated into a better language; and every chapter must be so translated...As therefore the bell that rings to a sermon, calls not upon the preacher only, but upon the congregation to come. So this bell calls us all, but how much more me, who am brought so near the door by this sickness...No man is an island, entire of itself...any man's death diminishes me, because I am involved in mankind; and therefore never send to know for whom the bell tolls; it tolls for thee." John Donne (1572-1631)

We are all joined together in our condition of humanity. We have one Creator. We all have one condition—created humanity. We all have one calling—Bride of Christ.

What happens to one of us affects all of us. We need each other. No one person can do everything alone. To get anything done in our life, we will always need the help of someone else. It is the way we were made.

We all need that comfort from someone else. In fact, an experiment done with a group of Korean babies showed that the babies who had just 15 minutes of voice, massage and visual stimulation gained more weight, more body length, and head circumference than those who did not receive the stimulation. And the opposite response was found in communist Romanian orphanages. Babies left alone except for very minimal necessary care did not thrive, and many died.

Skin to skin touch between mother and child has been shown to increase the physical development of the child as well as increase their ability to develop a relationship with people. Touch has been proven to reduce stress, relieve pain, increase the ability to cope with situations and improve general health.

Therapeutic touch has proven to lessen the symptoms in fibromyalgia, Alzheimer's and dementia.

We need each other at the very fundamental core of our beings. We were created to work together.

The more we connect as one, the more humanity will increase in compassion and love for one another. United we stand. Unified we cannot be divided.

This is why the Holy Spirit gives people different gifts as is His desire (Hebrews 2:4). He does this so we will work together, depending on each other's strengths. One of the last prayers of Jesus was that we should become one as the Godhead is one (John 17:11).

John says more on the subject of loving one's brother. And since we are all descended from the same people, we are all sisters and brothers. Whether you believe that we have descended from Adam and Eve, or from Noah, his sons and their wives, or the DNA which proves we are all from the 10 sons and 18 daughters of Eve, it all comes down to one thing: we are all related, skin and all.

John unequivocally states that unless we love our brother, we are not of God, we are dead. (1 John 3:10, 14, 17, 4:20-21) And for a little bit of encouragement, a hug burns off 35 calories in 30 minutes.

We live in community. It is sad that so many of us have forgotten that, with the rise of crimes, gangs, and violence at paramount levels in every country on earth. Everyone is out for themselves because we feel so alone and isolated. They have forgotten that to hurt someone else is to hurt a part of oneself because we are all joined, one to another.

From the richest to the poorest—we are all one, brother, sister, family.

We were created to live in community. The need to be loved and accepted is the greatest human need and its lack of fulfillment is at the root of all human violence. It leads to the need for power, wealth and fame in a feigned attempt to fill that void.

In fact, the way to get restored to health involves getting help from the repair guys, the community. We need to go to those who have pioneered in preparing raw food recipes. We need to go to an Upper Cervical Chiropractor to get our heads put on straight. We need to go to someone for help with inner healing and deliverance. We need to go to a gym or a swimming pool to get exercise. And we need support from friends and family.

We need community and there is no way around being part of the community. It is the sum of the law—love your neighbor as yourself (Mark 12:30-31).

CHAPTER 10: PRAYER

There is prayer and there is prayer.

So many people think that prayer is ritual...a set amount of time every day to list off a series of desires and demands. Their prayer is formal, habitual and full of repetition each and every single time.

Try talking to your friend that way. The friendship won't last for long.

Prayer is being in relationship with the God who created us and desires us all the time. Talking to Him is the same as talking to your spouse, your parent or friend.

There is nothing complicated or even formal about it. He cares. He always has. He always will. He was there before the moment of our conception and He will be there beyond the moment of our passing from this realm to the next. Someone that close deserves a relational attitude and frame of mind – honor, love, respect.

That is one of the things Jesus came to teach us. He had a relationship with Yahweh. Where others feared to mention His name, Jesus called Him *Abba, Father.*

Our Father in heaven! May Your name be kept holy. May your

Kingdom come, your will be done on earth as in heaven. Give us the food we need today. Forgive us what we have done wrong, as we too have forgiven those who have wronged us. And do not lead us into hard testing, but keep us safe from the Evil One. For kingship, power and glory are yours forever. (Matthew 6:9-13 CJB)

The prayer is simple. The prayer is straightforward relationship. We are as concerned about God as He is about us.

He is our Father who lives in heaven. We want His name to be kept holy, His reputation to be kept unblemished. We want His kingdom, not ours; we want His will not our way. Only after establishing that relationship, do we ask for what we need today—food, forgiveness, a forgiving heart, easy tests and to be kept from the Evil One. Then we close, still in relationship, giving Him the kingship, power and glory—His place, His authority, His right.

It is the same basis of every friendship. We care about them, they care about us, we care about them again.

Nothing could be simpler. So why do so many people try to make it a ritual and ceremony, a contest of who can recite the most scripture?

He is the God who created every cell in our body. He made us with such an intricate design. We needed to learn how to spiritually deal with that design, so He made a city in our likeness and called it Jerusalem. Prayer in the Holy of Holies takes place in the temple of the Lord, which is the temple we are. And The Holy of Holies is within us. Prayer should touch every facet of our life. Prayer should touch every step of our healing, deliverance, UC spinal correction, community...every step of our way.

We pray in our hearts, with our minds and with our mouths (hands for some). We pray regardless of the situation we find ourselves in, honestly and humbly. Then our prayers will be heard and answered.

CHAPTER 11: PUTTING IT ALL TOGETHER

We are the city of God, the place of His habitation. And, like the Levites, we must tend the temple 24/7.

That does not mean spending thousands of dollars on potions and capsules that rape the earth of acres of plants or hundreds of animals to make some concentrated form of magic cure-all. It means to eat as naturally as possible, keeping ourselves relatively free from chemicals, preservatives and contaminants.

That does not mean spending thousands of dollars on therapy and conferences but it does mean to take out the garbage; remove the garbage from inside your city through the dung gate personally. No one has authority over you except you, and it is with the authority of Jesus that we can evict that garbage to the pit outside the city walls.

That does not mean spending thousands on medical treatments or alternative medical practices or even subjecting ourselves to 35 surgeries. It does mean to get our heads on straight so that the brain stem is not compressed and the messages between the body and brain flow freely. It does not mean spending thousands on endless procedures, but it does mean spending the money necessary to free oneself of communication problems. This does have an end. I wish I had known about Upper Cervical Chiropractic corrections when I was born. Ok, at least when I was a lot younger, as it would have saved me 56 years of misery, expense and much decreased quality of life.

It does not mean spending thousands chasing after other people for answers, but instead, developing a relationship with God personally. It means seeking answers for ourselves and receiving them.

I will share a story here. My friend did not discern the voice of God. She has been on her face before the Lord desperately seeking answers. She prays in tongues, still did not feel sure He was speaking to her personally. She has sought, pleaded, asked and cried out to hear. It has caused her much distress. I have laid hands on her as have others, and still, God seemingly remained silent towards her. And yet, this is contrary to many words she has been given that said He spoke to her constantly.

Well, only a couple of weeks after her first Upper Cervical correction she began telling me things the Lord was speaking to her!!! Not only talking to her but she could hear Him laughing. It has become common place. He spoke to her continually, but after the UC correction took the compression off her brain stem, she began to hear what was always there—the voice of God speaking to her.

I hope this little book has helped you realize who you are in Christ and that you are the Temple of God. I hope this little book encourages you on the right path to healing and full health and your search brings you all the benefits of the Lord. I hope this little book brings you emotional, physical and spiritual freedom.

God bless you all,
Jessica and Susan

> Psalm 103.3-5 He forgives all your offenses, He heals all your diseases, He redeems your life from the pit, He surrounds you with grace and compassion, He contents you with good as long as you live, so that your youth is renewed like an eagle's.

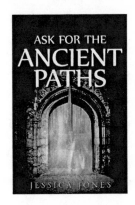

Ask for the Ancient Paths is an amazing, life-changing vision that takes you on the journey from before time to the end of this age. It shows how the jealousy of one angel forever marred the life of every angel and man alike.

This vision reveals aspects of three heavens, hell and angels that will forever change the way you look at the supernatural world. Follow through this Holy Spirit-inspired journey of how choices and agendas in the spirit realm have influenced and misdirected our path away from the perfect plan of God for His bride.

In order to find our way back into the incredible intimacy of relationship with God the Father, our Creator, it is essential to understand what went wrong.

Discover the truth about the subtleties of sin from the pers-pective of the Godhead.

Lucifer had it all but decided to take what belonged to everyone else.

The Lord says, "It's enough! It's time to take back what is rightfully the inheritance of the Body of Christ."

The Ancient Path is there to be discovered and enjoyed. And He wants you back on it towards Him, and the life, rewards and privilege He bought back for you on the cross.

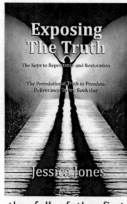

Exposing the truth compares the heart of God to the reality of present day Christianity.

Exposing The Truth examines how far we have fallen from the life and world God intended for His Bride. It documents the progress of continual falling of man after the fall of the first man! Studying God's plan for His Creation, we then can see what has followed throughout the 6,000 years. The misconceptions, the lies that have shaped our lives on earth. Even as Christians we struggle to keep our relationship with God alive, and especially to move into a deeper relationship with Him. Christians struggle to keep those communication lines open, believing God must not be on the job, when in reality, the problem is our lack of understanding or knowledge of our Father, God.

This book endeavors to break out of the boxed-in mindset we have inherited…not our Godly inheritance, but our satanic inheritance. It looks into the varied world structures of our current societies, attempting to expose the truth of their origins. By Exposing the Truth in relation to our current life situation regardless of our geographical roots, it becomes evident how far off the mark of Christ Jesus we have traveled. It's time to get back on track.

Printed in the United States
146070LV00005B/1/P

9 780981 454801